Who Says a Pickle Has to be Green?

By
Linda T Carlson

Illustrated by Hatice Bayramoglu

Who Says a Pickle Has to be Green?

Copyright: 2021 Linda T.Carlson

Written By: Linda T.Carlson

Illustrations, layout and typesetting: Hatice Bayramoglu

Dedicated to
Courtney, Anthony, Hannah, Adrianna, Isaiah, Allison,
Alexander, Samuel, Jase, Isaac, and Levi

Have you ever seen a real purple pickle?

In Mr. Ficklestein's deli,
you can buy one for a nickel!

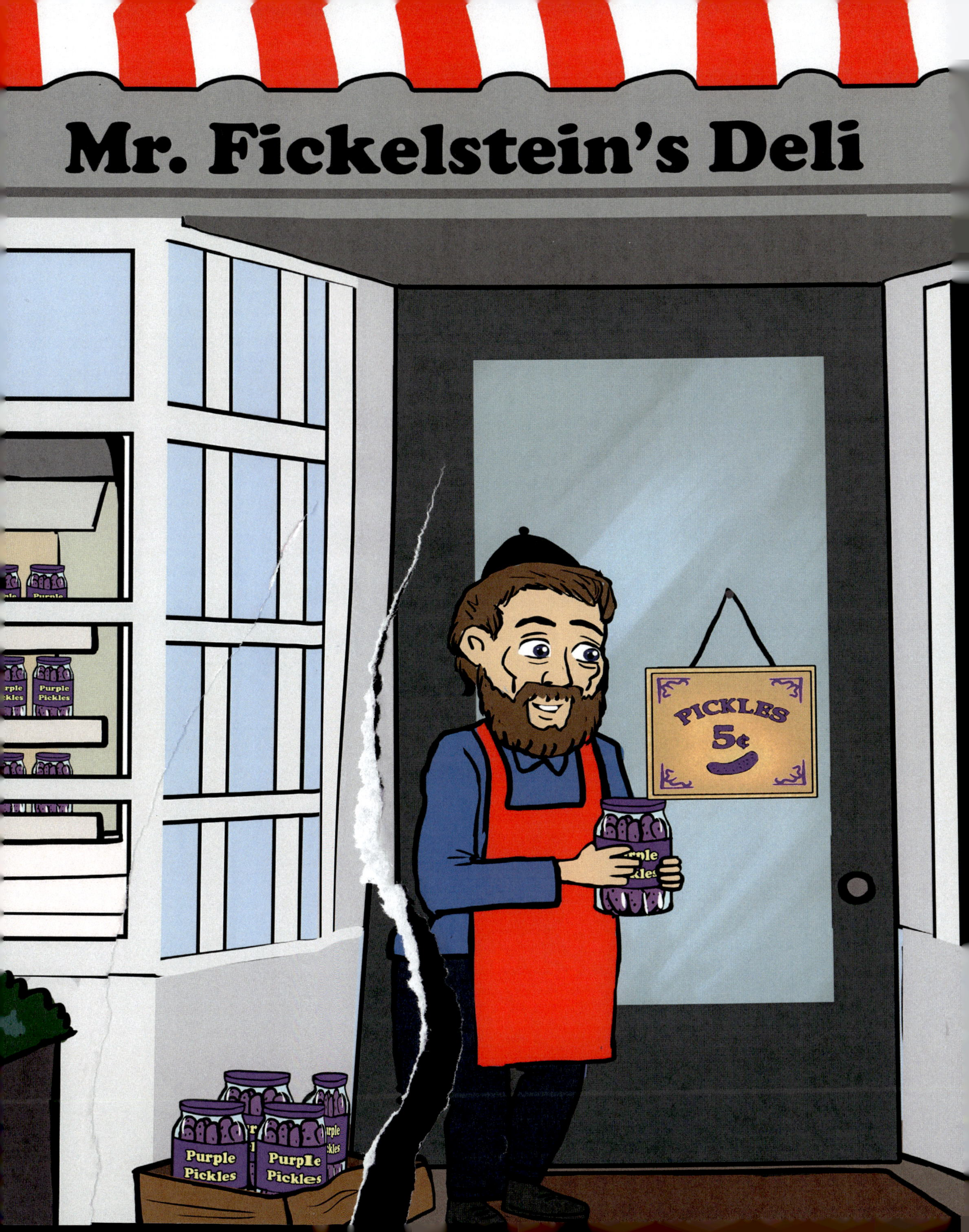
Mr. Fickelstein's Deli
PICKLES
5¢
Purple Pickles
Purple Pickles
Purple Pickles

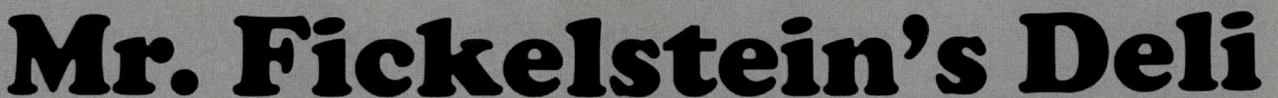

My name is Sam and this is my cousin A.J. I can't wait to bring him to the deli.

Look at all the purple pickles, see what I mean!

Well, now the secret's out..

Not every pickle is green!

"There's something else you
need to know
about these purple pickles!"
said Mr. Ficklestein.

I suppose you want to taste one, they're very much unique.

So crispy and crunchy,
delicious as a treat!

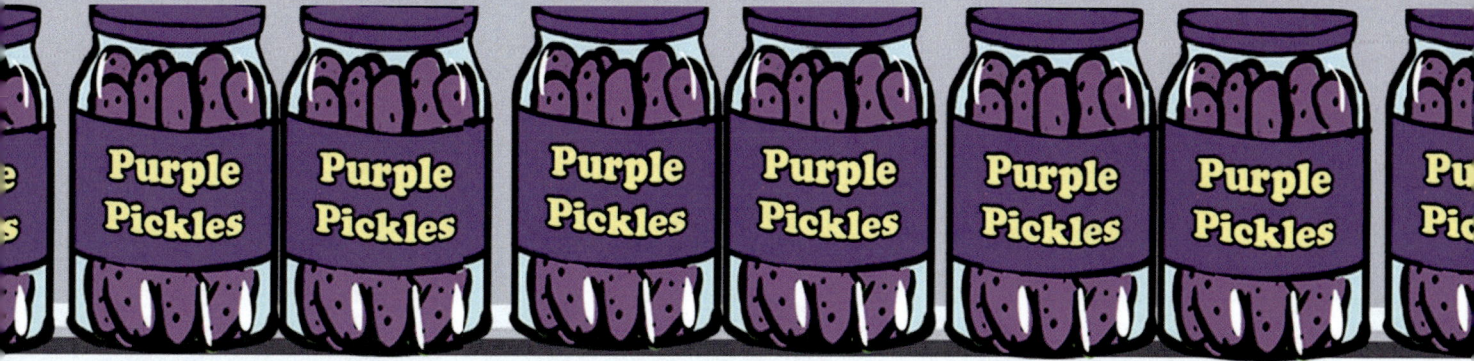

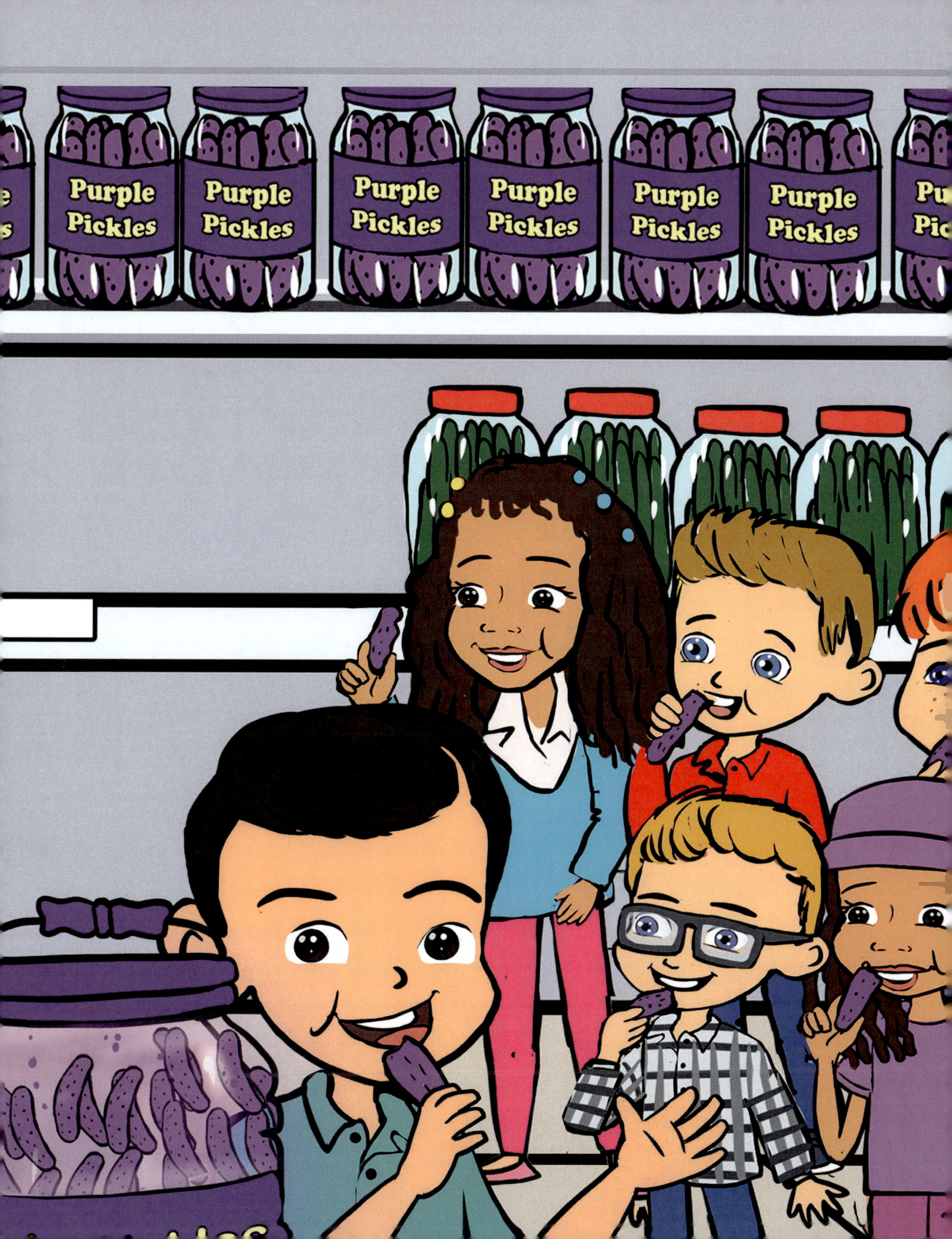
Purple Pickles
Purple Pickles
Purple Pickles
Purple Pickles
Purple Pickles
Purple Pickles

And just like the green ones, they come in dill or sweet!

Mommy says my purple pickles keep me very strong.

And Dr. Wickle says I'm the perfect height, right where I belong!

Dr. Wickle whispered, "Have you been eating purple pickles?"

"How did you guess?"

I heard it through the grapevine that they sell for just a nickel!

My teacher, Ms. McGill
says I'm doing really fine.

She said there must be something magical in that purple pickle brine!

It's true these purple pickles are almost never seen.

It's time we ask the question…

Who says a Pickle Has to be Green?

Made in the USA
Columbia, SC
16 February 2023

12219813R00027